The Nature Club
Racing with Butterflies

This book is a work of fiction.

Edited by Emma Irving and Julie Mazur Tribe

A portion of the proceeds from the sale of this book will benefit butterfly conservation.

Library of Congress Cataloging-in-Publication Data is available upon request.
ISBN 978-1-7329156-1-9 (paperback)
ISBN 978-1-7329156-6-4 (ebook)

First edition 2019

10 9 8 7 6 5 4 3 2 1

Wild Bear Press operates on the simple premise that nature-based stories connect children with the natural world and inspire them to protect it.

Visit us on the Web! www.natureclubbooks.com

The Nature Club

Racing with Butterflies

Rachel Mazur

For Sophie, Spencer, and Curtin,
with gratitude and admiration

1

As Tai rode his horse, Dune, he imagined the outcome of the barrel racing competition at next weekend's Green County Rodeo. *And this year's blue ribbon goes to Tai Davis!*

Tai had won two years in a row in his hometown in Nebraska and then missed last year's rodeo when he moved west with his dad. Dune would soon be too old to race, but, for now, he was strong and fast. *If I win this rodeo,* Tai thought, *I can retire Dune as a local champion.*

Lost in thought, Tai arrived home, unsaddled Dune, and gave him a good brushing. He didn't even hear his father, who had walked out to join him. "How was practice?" Tai's dad asked, handing Dune a bunch of sweet hay.

"I beat my best time," Tai responded with a bit of swagger. "Just a hair under sixteen seconds."

"That's my boy," his dad commended, with a huge grin. "You're going to teach these local cowboys how to ride!"

"I sure hope so—with Dune's help," Tai replied, feeling inside his pocket for his lucky penny. "You know, Izzy and Brooke have never seen a barrel race before. I want to win it with them watching."

Tai released Dune into the pasture while his dad hung his saddle, harness, and tack. When they were done, Tai wiped his brow and leaned against an old cottonwood tree.

He rested for a moment and then broke into a broad grin and jumped into a puddle. As he did, dozens of light-blue butterflies scattered about.

"What're all these butterflies doin'?" Tai asked his dad as he chased them.

"Those butterflies," his dad explained, "are puddling."

"Are what?"

"They're puddling," his dad laughed. "Butterflies gather together and rest on puddles of mud, urine, or even dung to drink water and absorb salts."

"What's dung?" Tai asked.

"You know," his dad responded. "Dung is poop. They don't like the dry, round kind we refer to as 'horse apples'—they're more into the wet, mushed-up kind."

"Oh. Gross," Tai observed.

"I suppose that's true for a human. But butterflies see the world differently," Mr. Davis said. "Come here. I want to show you something you'll like."

They walked to the edge of their pasture and Mr. Davis knelt down. "Take a look at these milkweed plants."

"Why?"

"Because there's a great partnership between milkweeds and one of the most famous butterflies in the land. You can observe it right here if you look closely."

Tai bent down to study a milkweed, and, on it, he saw a large caterpillar banded with black, yellow, and white horizontal stripes. It was busily chewing through a wide, green leaf.

"Oh, good," Mr. Davis said. "You found a monarch caterpillar. Also known by its Latin name, *Danaus plexippus*."

"Dana what?" Tai asked.

"*Danaus plexippus*."

"How about we call her Dana for short?" Tai suggested.

"Fine with me," his father said. "Once Dana goes through metamorphosis, she'll become a beautiful monarch butterfly. You know what metamorphosis is, right?"

"We learned about it in school. It's when something changes form. With butterflies, an egg becomes a larva—and that's the caterpillar. Then the caterpillar becomes a pupa—and that's the chrysalis. And last, the chrysalis becomes an adult—and that's the butterfly."

"Right. In goes a caterpillar and out comes a butterfly," Mr. Davis said.

"Are these monarch eggs?" Tai asked, pointing

to tiny green balls on the leaf.

"Oh no. That's frass from your caterpillar," answered his dad. "Caterpillar poop," he clarified when he saw Tai's puzzled expression. "The eggs are off-white and tiny. They could fit on the head of a pin." As he talked, he searched a milkweed plant. "Monarchs almost always lay them on the undersides of milkweed leaves. In fact," he paused and pointed to a spot on one of the leaves, "there's one right here. If you look closely, you'll see it's covered in ridges."

Tai examined the egg while his father explained what would happen next. "Within a week, a tiny caterpillar will chew a hole through the egg and work its way out. Then it'll eat and grow continuously—a lot like you these days."

Tai looked up from the egg to make a face at his dad.

Mr. Davis made a face back and continued. "Every few days it will pause to molt—or to shed its skin—so it can keep growing larger until, after about two weeks, it will be over two thousand times bigger than it was when it began."

"Not like me," Tai said.

His dad laughed. "Let's hope. Anyway, each period of time the caterpillar has a new skin is called an 'instar.' Based on Dana's size, banding pattern, and a few other traits, I'm pretty sure she's in her fourth instar.

"The fifth instar is the final one. When she's done growing, she'll find a sheltered spot under a branch to pupate. By pupate, I mean transform into a butterfly. Monarchs do this in an amazing-looking chrysalis. I'll try to find you one . . ." Mr. Davis stopped talking and focused on looking for a chrysalis for a few minutes.

"Hmm. I can't find one right now, but when it finally emerges between one and two weeks later, it'll look like . . ." Mr. Davis looked around, "like that butterfly there," and he pointed to a large, reddish-orange butterfly flying past, with wings that had striking black edges with white dots and a network of black lines within.

They watched the butterfly slowly sail about

for a few minutes until it landed on a coneflower.

"I thought you said they only use milkweed," Tai said.

"Milkweed is the only plant monarch butterflies lay their eggs on, and once the caterpillars emerge, milkweeds are the only plants they'll eat. Once they are adults, however, they use milkweeds and other plants for nectar."

"Are there a lot of different kinds of milkweeds?" Tai asked.

"I can tell you about butterflies," his dad, who was an expert on all things bird and butterfly said, "but if you want to know more about the plants, you're going to have to ask your mother. She's the best botanist—and the best dentist—I know."

"But she isn't here," Tai said, kicking the dirt with his boot. His parents had separated just over a year ago, right before Tai and his father had moved west. When they had moved, his mother immediately flew to Japan to visit her parents, and since then, had remained in Nebraska. Although Tai had gone back four times to visit her, she hadn't yet come out to Greenley, California, to see where he was living.

"Well, actually," his father said, "I've got a surprise for you."

"Mom's coming?!" Tai asked, his face lighting up.

"She is. She's coming to see you race."

"Next week?" Tai asked, his face now glowing with anticipation.

"She arrives tomorrow and will stay a full week, leaving the following Sunday."

"Awesome! Is she staying with us?" Tai asked hopefully.

"You know that's not realistic," his father answered, "but she'll be right down the street at the Clementine Inn. Now, come on, let's go inside for dinner." Mr. Davis put his arm around his son and they walked to the house together. "It'll be good to see her," he added.

As they entered the house, Tai could smell his dad's specialty, lasagna, and was filled with hope. *My dad is looking forward to seeing my mom*, he thought. *Once they look at each other, they'll remember how much they like each other and . . .*

But then, as he entered the kitchen, Stephanie, his father's girlfriend, walked over. "Hey, Tai," she said, innocently shattering his daydream.

2

Just as Tai sat down to start eating, Dana finished eating. Only she wasn't stopping to rest, she was stopping to shed her skin, for she had grown so much that it was now too tight. At first, she made pulsing movements with her body and then full contractions. Finally, she wiggled free of the tight outer layer of her old skin and walked away in the bright layer of new skin that had grown in below.

She was now in her fifth and final instar—the last one before pupating into a butterfly. To bulk up one last time, she used her tiny antennae to smell for another leaf and then moved toward it in rippling movements. Dana walked by taking one step forward with her rear pair of legs followed by one step by the pair just in front of those, and on and on until it was time to step forward with the rear pair again.

In truth, her five pairs of rear legs were false legs called prolegs. Only her front three pairs were true legs. But they all served the purpose of movement, and she wiggled her black front and back tentacles to feel her way as she went.

Dana crawled onto the new milkweed leaf and busied herself clipping off the tiny hairs covering the leaf. When she finished, she set about draining the sticky white latex from the leaf.

During Dana's first instar, she was so tiny that she could have died if she had gotten stuck in the latex. To avoid it, she chewed circular patterns in leaves before she ate them to allow the latex to seep out. Now that she was bigger, she simply had to bite a big chunk out of the leaf's stem to let the latex drain.

With her new leaf ready, Dana used all of her front three pairs of true legs to hold the leaf steady and got busy eating. Nibbling back and forth, back and forth, she crunched through it.

It was exactly a year ago that Dana's great-grandmother had spent her days as a caterpillar crunching through milkweed leaves in this very field during her one-month life. Dana's great-grandmother had never left the field, but once she was a butterfly, she used her energy to lay eggs, one of which would become Dana's grandmother—and Dana's grandmother's life would be different.

Unlike Dana's great-grandmother, once Dana's grandmother was a butterfly, she used her energy to migrate all the way to the California coast—or possibly even as far as Mexico—before winter. It was an astounding navigational feat given that she had never been there before. There, she spent her days gorging on nectar for energy, and she spent her nights clinging to the leaves of a eucalyptus tree, huddled with hundreds of other monarchs for warmth.

Then in March, when the days grew warmer, Dana's grandmother started migrating back toward the Davises' pasture. Dana's grandmother lived nine months, much longer than the one-month Dana's great-grandmother had lived, but still, one day on the trip north, she became exhausted and stopped to lay eggs on roadside milkweeds before she died.

Dana's mother came from one of those eggs. Once Dana's mother was a butterfly, she continued the journey north until she got back to the Davises' pasture, another astounding navigational feat given she had never been there before. When she arrived, she laid eggs and collapsed in exhaustion. One of her eggs became Dana.

Dana, like her great-grandmother, would end up spending her entire one-month life in that same pasture. And one day, toward the end of her life, Dana would lay her own eggs. The butterflies that would be born from those eggs would, like Dana's grandmother, live a much longer life than Dana and migrate all the way to the California coast or Mexico for the winter.

But Dana knew none of that, nor did she care. She was focused solely on crunching through milkweed leaves.

3

The next afternoon, Tai was riding Dune around the Davises' pasture when his dad called out to him, "Tai! She's here! Your mom's here!"

Tai rode up to the house while his dad walked out to meet him. "Where is she?" Tai asked eagerly.

"She's at the hotel. She's coming to pick you up in fifteen minutes. Why don't you take a quick shower and pack an overnight bag to stay with her tonight? I'll take care of Dune."

"Thanks, Dad. Can you give Dune extra oats? He seems tired. Maybe I ran him too hard yesterday."

"Sure thing," said Mr. Davis.

Tai then asked tentatively, "Are you excited to see Mom, too?"

His father paused, "Your mother is a wonderful

person, and it'll be great to see her." He then added, "Now go on and get ready."

Tai, grinning, turned and ran into the house.

Exactly fifteen minutes later, Tai's mom pulled up in front of the house in a blue convertible. She wore a bright-red sweater and had her thick black hair—so similar to Tai's—pulled back in a bun. Tai ran out, threw his bag into the backseat, jumped over the front door, and landed in the seat next to her. "You're finally here!" he said, greeting her with a big hug.

"Oh, Taiyo-kun, how I've missed you," she responded, hugging him back.

Tai smiled. His mother was the only person who called him by his full name, Taiyo. Since his mother was born in Japan, she had given him a Japanese name to connect him to her homeland. She had chosen "Taiyo," which means "big world," because he had one parent from the United States and the other from far-away Japan. Like many Japanese mothers, she then added "kun" to the end of his name as a term of endearment.

Tai's mom held him at arm's length to look him over. "You are tall for a ten-year-old!"

"Dad does feed me," Tai smiled. "Want to see him? He's in the pasture."

Tai pointed to his dad, and his mom looked over and waved. Tai hoped his dad would walk over and greet his mother, but Mr. Davis, who was busy cleaning out Dune's hooves, didn't move from his spot. He just waved and called out, "Hello, Suki."

"Hello, Dustin," responded Tai's mom, also not moving from her position in the convertible. Then she yelled, "Don't you worry about Tai. I'll take great care of him!"

"I know you will. Have fun, you two. I'll see you tomorrow."

"Bye, Dad!" Tai added, his stomach knotting in disappointment. This wasn't going as he'd imagined.

Tai's mother, however, quickly distracted Tai by starting the engine and asking, "What do you think of this car?"

"It's a lot more fun than Dad's old pickup truck. Is it yours?"

"It is for the week! Let's have an adventure. What do you want to show me?"

That question was easy to answer. If there was one place Tai loved more than any other, it was Green County Park. But his town was small, and he decided to save the best for last. First, he took his mother to see the riding arena, then down Main Street, and after that, he showed her his school. Next, he brought her to his karate school, also called a dojo.

"Let's stop at my dojo," Tai suggested. "I want you to meet Master Takumi."

It was locked, but they could still peek through the front window. "Wow. There are so many mats. I bet you have a good time knocking down the other kids," his mother joked.

"Sparring is a lot of fun," Tai admitted, "but I also really like practicing the Universal Forms—especially the ones with the bokken."

"Let me guess, the bokken is some kind of

weapon, right?" his mom asked.

"It's actually a wooden training sword."

"Your grandfather would be so proud of you," his mother sighed. "When you are ready to get that black belt, you know I'll be in the front row watching."

"Maybe you can practice push-ups with me to prepare. I'll have to do a hundred to earn it."

"Uh . . . maybe," his mom laughed. "Now how about you take me to that park you've been telling me about?"

"Green Meadow!" Tai exclaimed. "Let's go!"

"Excellent!" proclaimed his mother. They climbed back into the car, and she let Tai guide her back through town and toward Green Meadow.

Ten minutes later, they pulled into a small gravel parking lot looking out on a creek and a beautiful meadow. "Are we already there?" his mom asked.

"We are. It's a small town," Tai explained. "Welcome to Green County Park!"

"What a gorgeous place," she commented, getting out of the car. "The meadow is so lush, and I love all the willows along the edge!"

"We'll also come here tomorrow for a picnic with my friends."

"Great! I can't wait to meet your friends."

"This is where we spend most of our time, and it's where Dad studies birds. He bands here, does point counts here—he even does his fall hawk migration watch here."

His mother smiled. "I have such good memories of early mornings out studying birds with your father. We had so many laughs and would always start by sitting and watching the sunrise . . . ," her voice trailed off as she was momentarily lost in thought.

"We really miss you," Tai said, shifting his weight from one foot to the other.

"Oh, how I've missed you, Taiyo-kun," his mother responded, hugging him tightly. Straightening, she asked, "Do you remember Chloe? She was your father's assistant for several years back in Nebraska."

"She always brought hot chocolate with marshmallows for me," Tai said.

"That's right," remembered his mom. "I would put you in the car in your pajamas because we would leave so early in the morning and you would sleep until we pulled up to the research site. Then you would perk right up when you saw Chloe because you knew she had a thermos of hot chocolate for you. Who helps your dad with his research now?" she asked.

"Cody. He works with Dad and they do bird surveys together. He's great. You can meet him tomorrow," Tai offered.

"Aren't we having a picnic with your friends tomorrow?"

"We are, but Dad and Cody will be here banding, too."

Tai's mom looked at him sideways. "Does your dad know about this?"

"Well . . . ," Tai paused and stuffed his hands in his pockets. "He'll love it."

"Tai. That's not what I asked," she said gently, putting her hands on the sides of his face so she could look him in the eye.

"You don't have to spend a lot of time together. Just say hi and then we'll have a picnic at the other side of the meadow. Okay?" Tai pleaded.

"Okay," she agreed reluctantly and then, changing topics, said, "I brought you some *omiyage*." Tai's mother loved the Japanese tradition of giving gifts after being apart. She presented Tai with a handmade quilt, some new clothes, and a framed photograph of the two of them from when Tai was first born.

"This is the best," he said, looking at the photo.

Tai's mom hugged him tightly, saying, "I'm so glad you like it." Then she quickly wiped a tear from her eye and cleared her throat. "I want to take you out to dinner. Where should we go?"

"How 'bout pizza?" Tai recommended.

"Pizza it is." Tai and his mom got back into the car to head off for pizza and a movie before returning to the Inn and falling into a deep sleep.

4

When Tai woke up, his mother was sitting by the window. "I'm awake," he said groggily.

"Good morning," she replied. "How did you sleep?"

"Good, but I'm still tired."

"You slept for eleven hours. Isn't that enough?" his mom laughed.

Tai sat bolt upright. "What time is it? Did we miss the picnic?"

"On no. It's only nine a.m. We have plenty of time. Let's have breakfast and go to the pool until it's time to go."

Tai, who loved staying at hotels for their pools, jumped out of bed and put on his swimsuit. In no time, he and his mother were headed to the breakfast room and then out to the pool. They mostly swam but ended with a cannonball competition. Tai had more style, but his mom could make a bigger splash. After another hotel guest declared Tai the winner, they decided it was time to get ready for the picnic.

"Let's get sandwiches at Green Deli," Tai said. "It's on the way."

"That sounds perfect," his mom replied as they walked out to the car.

When they arrived at Green Meadow, the others were already there. They had come early to watch Tai's dad and his assistant, Cody, do a bird survey. As Tai and his mom got out of the car, Tai spotted Izzy and Brooke from across the meadow. "Hoo-ooo," he hooted.

"Hoo-oo-ooo," Brooke hooted back, waving and motioning for them to come on over.

"Come on, Mom, let's go!" Tai said, leading her in their direction.

His mom, following hesitantly, asked, "You did tell your father I'm coming, right?"

Tai pretended he didn't hear her and just said, "Come on, it'll be great."

Brooke pulled Izzy to run and meet Tai and his mother. "Hi, Tai," Brooke said. "We just finished the bird survey. Is this your mom?" she asked. Before he could answer, she turned to Tai's mom. "Hi Mrs. Davis. I'm Brooke and this is Izzy. We are so happy to meet you."

Izzy, who hung behind her more extroverted friend, fidgeted with her ponytail and said quietly, "Nice to meet you."

Tai's mom gave them each a warm hug. "I'm so happy to meet the two of you. And please, just call me Suki."

Tai frowned and kicked the dirt. "But her last name is Davis . . . just like my dad," he said.

Suki glanced at her son and smiled, saying, "That's true, but I'm becoming less formal."

"Cody is less formal, too," Brooke said. "He just goes by Cody. But we call Tai's dad, 'Mr. Davis'."

Suki laughed and changed the subject. "Tai has told me all about the Nature Club. It sounds terrific." Turning to Izzy, she then added, "He also tells me you moved to Southern California last winter but are now back, is that correct?"

"Well," Izzy began quietly, "we meant to move there for good, but my mom found a way for us to come back to Greenley for the summer. We'll go back for sixth grade."

"What an exciting life you live!" Tai's mom responded, making Izzy smile.

Right then, Tai's dad and Cody walked up. "Hello Suki," said Mr. Davis.

"Hello Dustin," she replied. "You look well." They shook hands awkwardly.

"I'd like you to meet Cody," Tai's dad continued, "and, of course, Izzy and Brooke, whom it looks like you've already met. Cody, this is Tai's mom, Suki."

Suki kept her eyes on Dustin for a moment before shifting her gaze to Cody. "It's awfully nice to meet you," she said, extending her hand.

Cody shook it, responding, "Likewise," with a smile.

"Will you be joining us for a picnic?" Suki asked tentatively.

Cody, unsure of the plan, looked at Dustin questioningly. Dustin took a deep breath and said, "Not today. No. Not today. I've got plans. You all have a good time."

"Please, Dad," Tai broke in. "Please."

"It's okay with me if it's okay with you," added his mom.

"Well . . . okay," Mr. Davis relented. "Just for a little while."

Tai's face lit up, and he ran over to the old oak tree to spread out a picnic blanket. They had a great feast, and when they were done, Tai's mom brought out a surprise dessert—*daifuku*, a glutinous rice cake stuffed with sweet filling. When Izzy and Brooke looked at it hesitantly, she explained it was popular in Japan and that Tai had loved it since he was a child. They both tried it and liked it—sort of—but were fine to leave most of it for Tai, who couldn't get enough.

5

After lunch, the kids took out their nature journals to sketch and make notes. Tai decided to focus on the plants toward the edge of the meadow and walked over to check them out. "Hey, Dad!" he called. "Aren't those tall ones milkweed plants?"

"They are," Mr. Davis confirmed. "Let's look for monarch eggs and caterpillars."

The group, always curious about nature, joined them. While they searched, Mr. Davis explained to the group how to identify eggs, caterpillars, and adults.

Chiming in, Tai's mother asked, "Do any of you know another reason why the relationship between monarchs and milkweeds is so fascinating?"

"Is it because they're always together?" Brooke

asked her.

"Well, yes, but what's even more fascinating is that milkweed plants have a sap with sticky, milky-white latex and poisonous, bitter chemicals that few living things can eat. Monarchs, however, can avoid the latex while incorporating the poison into their own bodies to make them safe from predators. Many predators know these bright orange and black butterflies are poisonous and bitter and simply avoid them."

"Are you saying milkweed plants provide not only food for monarch caterpillars *and* shelter for monarch eggs, *but also* protection for monarch adults?" Izzy said in amazement. Tai's mom smiled and nodded.

"Are the other bugs we saw on the milkweed plants going to die?" asked Brooke.

"Those insects will be fine. They are going for nectar. It's just the sap of the milkweed that's poisonous. Other parts of milkweed plants are widely used. The nectar, for example, is sweet and provides a high-energy food for lots of insects,"

Tai's mom explained.

"And even some hummingbirds," his dad added. "Birds use the seed floss from the milkweed pods in their nests."

"The what?" Brooke asked.

"You know the big pod-like fruits that grow on milkweeds and split open in the fall to release huge globs of white fluff? That white fluff is attached to the milkweed seeds. It helps them blow in the wind to new places to grow into new plants," Mr. Davis explained.

"Dad calls the fluff 'floss,'" Tai added.

"In the past, people also used milkweed plants," his mom said. "Their parts have been used in food, medicine, cloth, and even life jackets."

"Mom," Tai broke in, "tell them about the monarchs' migrations."

"Butterflies migrate?" asked Brooke.

"They sure do," Tai answered confidently.

"Why don't you explain it?" his mother suggested.

Tai look at his mom with one eyebrow raised. "I don't know if I can do that, but I can tell you that it takes a lot of butterflies to get from their wintering grounds back to here in the spring."

His mom laughed and turned to Brooke. "Monarchs have a famous migration. The ones born east of the Rocky Mountains spend their winters in Mexico. The ones born west of the Rocky Mountains, like the ones here, spend their winters either along the California coast or in Mexico."

"Wow, that little butterfly has a long way to go," said Brooke.

"That's the really amazing thing," Tai's mom said. "That little butterfly won't be going anywhere. It will be its children or grandchildren that make the trip, and they will arrive at exactly the right place even though they've never been there before."

"I don't get it," Brooke said.

"It takes four generations of monarchs—give or take a few—to complete a full migration.

During the summer, a first generation of monarchs is born, lives its whole life, and lays its eggs before dying in the same place. From those eggs comes a second generation, but that generation flies all the way to Mexico or the California coast to spend the winter—even though it has never been there before. In the spring, that butterfly will fly part way back and lay its eggs before it dies. A third generation comes from those eggs, flies farther back, and lays its eggs and dies.

Finally, a fourth generation is born at that place, flies the rest of the way back, and lays its eggs before it dies, thus completing the cycle," Tai's mom explained. "Sometimes it even takes another generation for the monarchs to make their way back north."

"Whoa," Brooke commented. "How does anyone know that?"

"It took years of observations and a lot of patience for researchers to figure it out—and there is still a lot they are trying to learn. Since all the generations of butterflies look alike, the researchers caught butterflies and attached tiny stickers labeled with unique numbers on each butterfly. They then re-caught the butterflies in a range of other locations to figure it out."

"Imagine spending your whole summer catching butterflies!" Brooke said.

"I hope they were careful," Izzy added.

"Oh, yes, they were specially trained and very careful," Tai's mom answered.

"Here's another amazing piece of the puzzle," she continued. "The butterflies that migrate live nine months, and the ones that stay in one place only live for about one month."

"What? That would be like me living for over 800 years compared to the rest of you," Tai calculated.

"How do you know you'd be the one to migrate? Maybe it would be me," Brooke said.

Izzy looked at them, saying, "I think you are both crazy."

"And energetic," Tai's mom added. "The

butterflies that migrate south from the East Coast travel up to three thousand miles. That can mean up to fifty miles a day for a tiny insect."

"They migrate as far as a lot of birds!" Brooke exclaimed. "We learned that cats, windows, and habitat loss are some of the biggest threats to migrating birds. What are the biggest threats to migrating monarchs?"

Tai's mom took a deep breath. "Unfortunately, monarchs aren't doing well at all. They have problems on their wintering grounds, their stopover grounds, and even their breeding grounds."

"Oh no!" said Izzy, her eyes wide.

"In Mexico, the monarchs go to an area near Mexico City where they stay warm at night by roosting together in Oyamel fir trees. In California, they do the same, but in eucalyptus, cypress, or pine trees. In both of those places, a lot of the habitat has been lost to development and tree-cutting. In California, some of those areas are now protected, but others are completely gone. I don't know the status of the forests in Mexico."

"I'll ask my pen pal, Miguel," offered Izzy.

"I thought he lived in Nicaragua, not Mexico," said Tai.

"Right, but he keeps track of the status of conservation efforts all through Mexico and Central America. I think he'll know," she explained.

"Please let me know what he says," Suki said. "I'd love an update."

"What about the stopover points and breeding grounds?" Izzy asked. "Is it as awful as the story on the wintering grounds?"

"Actually, it's worse. A lot of fields that had nectar plants or milkweeds have been developed or converted to cornfields. The plants that remain are often contaminated with chemicals that are used to kill insects," Tai's mom answered.

Looking at the kids' faces, she then sighed. "I sound like 'Debbie-downer,' don't I?" The kids all nodded. "Listen, the situation is bad, but change is happening. For example, in the Midwest, Interstate 35 is now designated as the 'Monarch Highway,' to spread awareness. There are also many, many groups of people out planting milkweeds for the monarchs. Unfortunately, they got a bit of a bumpy start, but now I think they are making a difference."

"Bumpy? What kind of bumps?" Brooke asked.

"At first, many people were planting milkweed plants without thinking about the actual migration routes where the plants were needed. Other people were planting the wrong types of milkweed plants, and they were not meeting the monarchs' needs. I think now, though, that most of that is getting straightened out."

Izzy, still clearly distressed, asked quietly, "What can we do?"

"Good question! We *are* the Nature Club, after all," added Brooke enthusiastically.

"You know you always have the power to educate others. The more people know, the more they can participate. You can also write letters to your elected officials. But I'm a big fan of direct action. Right here, you can make sure local, native milkweed plants are protected."

As Tai's mom spoke, his dad smiled at her, listening closely. He had learned a lot from her over the years. Tai watched his father watch his mother and began to daydream while the conversation moved on to other topics. *They're getting comfortable around each other again. I bet Dad will ask Mom to have dinner with us, and they'll decide to get back together. She could move here before the end of the summer . . .*

"What do you think, Tai?" asked Izzy, nudging him.

Tai, shaken out of his thoughts, said, "Think about what?"

"Think about coming to my house for dinner tonight? Brooke already said she could come."

"Um . . . I think I'm busy," he answered, looking back and forth between his mother and his father.

"Actually, I think it's a good idea," his mother

piped in. "I need to spend a few hours making calls this afternoon while you practice for the Saturday race. It would then be easy for me to grab a salad at the hotel and pay some bills while you're at Izzy's."

"And Stephanie and I are going to take advantage of your mother being here and leave town for a few days. We'll come back Thursday," added his father, crushing Tai's hopes for a family reunion that evening or in the next few days.

"Oh . . . okay." He turned to Izzy, "I guess I can come over after practice."

"Great," said Izzy, looking sideways at Tai. "Come on over around five when my mom will be home from work."

"Then I'll pick you up back at your house at seven to take you to the hotel," added Tai's mom.

Tai grunted an "Okay," and kicked at the dirt with his boot. This was not the family reunion he had imagined.

6

Tai's mother left Green Meadow alone to return to the hotel, and Tai rode with his father back to their house. Tai sat silently in the back seat, clenching his teeth while trying to make sense of what just happened. *Mom and Dad seem like they like each other, so why does Dad still want to go out of town with Stephanie instead of having dinner with Mom?*

"You okay, Tai? Did you have a good visit with your mother?" his dad interrupted.

"Yeah," Tai responded sullenly.

"Do you want to come in and talk about it when we get home?" his dad offered.

"Thanks, but I'd better get in a practice ride with Dune," Tai replied. He wanted to talk to his dad, but he didn't know what to say. He also wanted to avoid Stephanie, whom he knew would be at the house.

"Okay, but Stephanie and I are leaving right away and will be gone until Thursday, so if you change your mind, call me anytime," his dad urged, parking the car in front of their house. "I'm sorry I didn't tell you earlier. We just decided on this trip last night."

"Yeah, whatever," Tai said flatly.

Mr. Davis gave Tai a warm hug despite the stiffness in his son's shoulders.

"See you Thursday," Tai mumbled, getting out of the car and heading toward the pasture. Out of the corner of his eye, Tai could see Stephanie emerging from the house with a suitcase and getting into the car with his dad. He waved stiffly as they pulled away.

Then Tai turned and walked straight to Dune. He hoped to get in a good practice session to prepare for Saturday and forget his worries. Dune, however, still seemed tired and was now coughing, too—he was in no condition for a big workout. Tai, feeling nothing was going his way, kicked a post in frustration.

When that did nothing but hurt his toe, he yelled into the sky, which started a chorus of dogs barking throughout the neighborhood, clearly upsetting an already uncomfortable Dune. “Don’t worry Dune, I’m here for you,” he said, scratching Dune’s neck. “The main thing we need is for you to get better.”

Tai’s neighbor, Mr. Garcia, who was working in his yard, spotted Tai and immediately walked over. Mr. Garcia, who rarely spoke to Tai, was a tall, broad-shouldered man who intimidated Tai by his very presence. “Tai,” he said, his voice loud and brash, “I’ve been watching that horse of yours all morning, and he doesn’t look good. My bet is he’s been eating those poisonous milkweeds. They will kill him if you don’t get rid of them.”

“What? Dune could die?” Tai exclaimed, a knot forming in his stomach.

“Oh, he can recover, as long as you get rid of those weeds.”

“But what about the monarch butterflies that

need them?"

"I don't know about monarchs. I only know about weeds, and those weeds are poisonous and need to go."

Tai's mouth dropped open, as he thought not only about his beloved horse being sick, but also about removing the one and only plant monarchs need to survive.

Mr. Garcia, patted Tai's shoulder, his voice softening. "I know hand-pulling is a lot of work, and you are getting ready for your big race Saturday. I could help you."

"No . . . it's not the work . . . it's just . . . ," Tai stalled.

"It's no problem," Mr. Garcia said. "I'll think about getting rid of the milkweeds and you think about winning your race."

"How'd you know I'm racing Saturday?" Tai interrupted.

"Come on, I see you practicing. You're good. Of course you're racing Saturday—and if you aren't, you should be! Hey, I tell you what: I started spraying the weeds around my yard last weekend. I plan to spray the rest early Friday. That's the day the county workers are scheduled to mow all the roadside plants. How about if I spray yours while I'm at it?"

Tai gulped and forced himself to speak. "Uh . . . wow . . . that's really nice of you," he stammered, "but I, uh, I need to ask my dad, and he just left town until Thursday."

"No need to ask your dad. I don't need any payment," Mr. Garcia clarified.

Tai, feeling reluctant but desperate for his horse to survive and afraid to say no to Mr. Garcia, nodded in agreement.

"Okay, then. It's a plan," Mr. Garcia said loudly. He turned abruptly and headed back to his house, stopping on the way to gather a handful of wildflowers. Tai had seen him doing this before and always thought it seemed strange for such a dominating man.

He'd once mentioned it to his dad, but his dad brushed him off, saying, "Tai, don't be ridiculous.

Just because he's a man doesn't mean he can't like flowers. And besides, his wife is in a wheelchair. Maybe he picks them for her."

Tai wanted to know why Mr. Garcia's wife was in a wheelchair, but his dad didn't know, and Tai was too scared to ask Mr. Garcia himself. Tai continued to think about it as he picked up a brush to untangle Dune's long mane.

Tai couldn't imagine living without Dune. Tai and Dune had been together since Tai was five. At that time, his family had been living in a small town in Nebraska where their neighbors owned a large ranch with several horses. The owners had been elderly, so Tai's parents had often gone over to help them. Whenever they did, they would bring Tai, and he would spend the whole time watching their horses. One day as a thank you, the neighbors gave Dune to Tai's family, and their teenage grandson taught Tai how to ride.

Tai had taken to Dune immediately. When Tai turned seven and his parents had started fighting, Tai would escape by going outside to brush Dune and keep him company. When Tai's parents finally separated a year later, Tai's dad wanted to sell Dune before he and Tai moved.

When Tai heard about it, he begged his dad to get a house with a pasture so they could keep Dune until his father agreed. *Dune is more than a horse: he's like a brother to me,* thought Tai. With a heavy sigh, Tai continued brushing his horse, whispering, "Dune, you have to get better. You just have to."

7

As Tai brushed Dune, out in the pasture, Dana was finally full after days of eating milkweed. She stopped eating and turned her attention to finding shelter for her final transformation. She walked in her rippling rhythm from plant to plant until she found a suitably shaded milkweed. She was completely unaware she had left the Davises' pasture and entered the Garcias' yard.

The plant was the last healthy milkweed in a cluster of plants growing along one edge of Mr. Garcia's yard. All the milkweeds beyond it had been killed by the chemicals Mr. Garcia had sprayed the week before.

This plant, however, hadn't been sprayed, and its green stalk swayed in the breeze. Dana crawled under one of the milkweed's leaves and used her mouth to spin a patch of silk onto the stem. Satisfied, she turned around and embedded hooks that grew from her back legs into the silk.

And then . . . she let go, remaining attached only by those back hooks. Although she was upside-down, Dana hung securely from the branch. She curled up her head and looked like a striped "J" hanging from the milkweed.

But the stripes didn't last long, for Dana started making pulsing movements, and, starting from behind her head, her skin split apart and continued to split all the way up her body until it was all clumped up near her rear back feet. Underneath that shed layer of skin wasn't a layer of newer skin as in previous instars—this time, what lay underneath was a green chrysalis.

Dana now looked something like a cap-less green acorn, and as the day passed, her chrysalis hardened and took on a deeper green color, and a row of golden dots appeared along the top. And that is where she would hang peacefully for the next two weeks.

8

Tai reluctantly left Dune at five o'clock to ride his bike to Izzy's house for dinner. When he got there, her mother answered the door. "Izzy's in the backyard with Zack. Would you like some fresh lemonade?"

"I sure would. Thank you," he answered, sitting on a stool nearby. While Mrs. Philips filled his cup, Tai started to relax. There was something about Mrs. Philips that made Tai comfortable and able to talk.

"Tai, what's wrong?" Mrs. Philips asked, noting the redness in his eyes.

"It's Dune," Tai said. "He's sick. My neighbor said it's from eating milkweed. He said Dune will be okay if I remove all the milkweed, but we won't be able to race on Saturday."

"Oh, I'm so sorry. I know you've been training

a long time for that race. Is your neighbor a horse expert or a veterinarian?"

"Oh no. He doesn't know about horses, but he knows a lot about weeds."

"Are you sure he's right?"

"What do you mean?"

"If he isn't experienced with horses, and he isn't a veterinarian, he could be wrong. Do you have a local veterinarian we can call?"

"Our usual veterinarian is gone for a month. The only other vet in town is . . ." he hesitated, ". . . is Stephanie."

"As in, your father's girlfriend?"

"Yeah."

"Well, what did she say?"

"I, uh . . . I haven't asked her."

"I know they're on the road, but don't you have her cell phone number?"

"Well, I do, but . . ."

"But what?"

"She'd get in the way," Tai said, looking away.

"Oh," Mrs. Philips said, looking at him more

closely. “How is your visit going with your mother?” she asked gently.

“It was going great until my dad left town with Stephanie.”

“But your mom is here to visit *you*, not your father.”

“But how will they get back together if they don’t spend time together?”

“Tai, this is a conversation you need to have with your mother. Tonight. Talk to her about how you feel about her and your dad. She doesn’t have to tell you how she feels, but at least then she will know how *you* feel. Then let her know you need to call Stephanie to ask about Dune.”

Tai sat quietly and then looked down, saying, “I just don’t know.”

Mrs. Philips stepped closer to Tai and looked him right in the face. “Every family is different with how much they share,” she said. “It is up to you if you want to try and talk about it, and it is up to your mom if she wants to talk about it, but at least if you bring it up, she will know it’s on your mind."

Right then, Brooke burst through the front door, and Izzy and her brother Zack appeared from the study.

"I thought you were outside," Mrs. Philips said.

"We were, but then I decided to check if Miguel wrote back, and he did!" Izzy announced excitedly.

"Really?" asked Brooke. "Usually it takes weeks for you two to write back and forth. Did you call him?"

"Actually, I emailed him. That's why we were back there—we were checking the email. I know what you're thinking—we normally only send each other hand written letters, but I made an exception this time to get back to Tai's mom."

"Cool. What did he know about the forest in Mexico?" Brooke asked.

"He said there was a huge amount of logging in the past, but it's not allowed anymore," Izzy answered.

"That's great!" Brooke said.

"The problem is," Izzy continued slowly, "after some big windstorms blew lots of trees over a few years ago, they decided to pull the fallen trees out instead of leaving them as habitat."

"That doesn't sound good," Brooke said.

"Right," Izzy agreed. "The butterflies are still losing habitat. But here is something. Miguel said drivers now have to go slower near the wintering areas to keep them from hitting the butterflies."

"Not just butterflies," Zack added. "*Rabbles* of butterflies." Zack, who hardly spoke, loved to tell them what groups of animals were called.

"Rabbles?" Brooke asked with her hands on her hips. "What are you talking about?"

"You know, rabbles. As in *swarms*. As in *lots* of butterflies," Zack answered.

"Interesting," commented Mrs. Philips. "When I think of cars hitting animals, I always think of deer. I never realized cars had such an impact on butterflies."

"That's why I ride my bike! To save the butterflies," boasted Tai, suddenly joining the conversation and making everyone laugh.

"Okay, team, let's sit down for dinner," announced Mrs. Philips.

The group had a lively conversation about all the benefits of riding bikes while sharing enchiladas and rice. Tai became so distracted from his worries that he lost track of time and had to bike quickly home to meet up with his mother. When he arrived, he only had time to run inside to grab a change of clothes and his lucky penny, which he shoved deep into his pocket.

As promised, Suki pulled up to get him right at seven. Tai was silent on the ride to the hotel, thinking about ways to open up the conversation with his mom. He finally decided to bring up Stephanie when they got to the room, as Mrs. Philips had suggested. Unfortunately, his nerves got the best of him. Instead, he blurted out, "Dune is sick, really sick!"

"What? Honey, what's going on?" his mother asked, looking concerned.

"Dune's tired and won't stop coughing.

Stephanie is the only veterinarian around right now, but I can't call her because she's such a problem."

"What do you mean? Does she yell at you or . . . ?"

"No, Mom, it's nothing like that. She's just in the way. She's in the way between you and Dad getting back together."

"Back together? Oh, Tai, we aren't getting back together. Our divorce will be final this summer."

"Divorce? But you had fun together this morning. He was listening to you, and you said you have good memories."

"Tai, your father and I have wonderful memories. And we will always be special to each other because we have you, but we will never get back together—and it has nothing to do with Stephanie. We decided to separate long before Stephanie came along."

"But if she went away, maybe you *would* get back together."

"Tai, when people marry, they marry because

they are in love, but to stay married, people must also like each other's company and be compatible. Good pairs bring out the best in each other. Your father and I loved each other, and at first we made a good match, but we changed. We morphed into different beings and needed new things. We were no longer a compatible pair."

"You don't *want* to get back together?" asked Tai.

"I really don't. Tai, it isn't just your father who has a new partner. I do as well."

"You do?"

"I do. His name is Chase, and you will meet him next time you visit. I am really happy. Chase brings out the best in me—just like you do when you and I are together. And your dad says Stephanie brings out the best in him."

"He does?"

"He does. And I like her."

"You've met her?"

"Just over the phone. We've talked several times to make sure we all take care of you as a team. And you know what? She's crazy about you, just like I am."

"But it's better when our family is together."

"Tai, I miss you desperately, and I'm going to find a way to be closer to you, but it won't be by going backward; it will be by moving forward. I need us all to be in positive, beneficial partnerships."

"You don't think she's horrible?"

"Not even a little bit. I think she's great for your father and great for you. I also think she's probably a very good veterinarian."

Tai didn't respond but simply sat closer to his mother and waited for her to continue.

"How about this? We will check on Dune first thing in the morning. If he isn't better, we will call Stephanie right away."

Tai didn't answer but hugged his mother tightly.

9

Tai and his mother woke early and had a quick breakfast before leaving the hotel to check on Dune. Despite their hopes, he wasn't better. He was coughing and tired, had clear liquid leaking from his eyes and yellow liquid leaking from his nose, didn't seem to have eaten, and clearly didn't have any energy.

Tai's mom pulled out her phone, dialed up Tai's dad, and handed the phone to Tai.

"Hello?" Dustin answered.

"Dad. It's Tai."

"Tai!" his father greeted him enthusiastically. Then, "Is everything okay?"

"It's Dune. He's sick. I need help. Can I talk to Stephanie?"

"Dune is sick? Of course you can talk to her," answered his father, handing the phone to

Stephanie.

"Tai?" asked Stephanie, surprised by his request.

"It's Dune. He's sick!" Tai blurted out.

"I can help you. Slow down and tell me everything," she said calmly.

Tai took a deep breath and told Stephanie about Dune's symptoms and about Mr. Garcia saying it was from the milkweed and how he planned to spray the milkweed.

"Okay, one thing at a time," said Stephanie. "First, we need to correctly diagnose Dune. How do you know he ate milkweed? Did Mr. Garcia actually see it?"

"No, but he said he knows a lot about weeds."

"Hmmm," she replied. "Can you go through his symptoms with me again?" Tai and Stephanie talked in detail about his symptoms until Stephanie finally said, "Have you noticed any other sick horses at the arena?"

"There was a horse named Golden Moon at the arena last week that seemed sick—she was coughing a lot, but she seems fine now, so it must have been something else."

"Or . . . ," Stephanie observed, "Golden Moon had a flu she passed on to Dune at the arena, and Dune has a sickness that has nothing to do with milkweed." She paused. "Here is what I want you to do," she said and then carefully described the treatment to Tai, finishing with, "It really comes down to rest and keeping him away from dust.

"But it doesn't mean *no* movement; make sure you get him walking every now and then to keep his blood flowing. And keep him away from other horses—I can't believe Golden Moon's owner took her to the arena while she was showing symptoms. Anyway, what it means is no practicing and no rodeo. I'm so sorry."

"I know," Tai said sullenly, "but Dune's health comes first. Does this mean it isn't milkweed poisoning?"

"I don't think it is, but to be sure, keep an eye out for these symptoms." Stephanie then listed a range of symptoms, starting with heavy drooling and ending with bloating and abnormal heart rate. "If you see any of those things, call me right away. If not, let's check in tomorrow morning. If Dune gets worse, we will come right home."

"Okay," was all Tai could say, followed by a loud exhale.

Tai's dad got back on the phone. "Tai, I'm so sorry about Dune and the rodeo. Please keep us posted, and we'll be right home if you need us."

"Dad?"

"Yes?"

"He'll be okay, right?"

"We will do everything in our power to make sure."

"Thanks, Dad," said Tai, his voice shaky. "I love you."

"I love you, too. Call if you need anything. You're in good hands with your mother."

Tai hung up the phone and told his mother the instructions he got from Stephanie. His mother listened intently and then said, "It sounds like we should pick up our stuff from the hotel so we can stay at your house tonight to keep a close watch over Dune."

Focused on the tasks ahead, Tai breathed more easily. After picking up their things and making a quick stop for lunch, they headed straight back to Dune. He was glassy-eyed and exhausted.

They rested with Dune in the shade all afternoon, passing the time reading to each other and playing cards. Then, suddenly, just before six o'clock, Dune whinnied and walked over to the trough for water. Tai and his mom looked at each other with their mouths hanging open. His mother stood up and remarked, "I wonder if he just needed rest."

"I think it was my lucky penny," Tai smiled slyly while patting his pocket.

"Whatever it was, let's take a break and make dinner," said his mom.

Feeling more energetic than they had all day, they went inside to make dinner together, returning to Dune afterward to keep him company. Tai's mom made a fire in the Davises' outdoor firepit, where they stayed warm and watched Dune move around more and more. When they finally left Dune at ten o'clock, they were confident he was recovering.

"Will you wake me up early so we can check on him?" asked Tai.

"Of course," his mom promised and hugged him. "It looks like he'll be okay."

"I think so. I feel so much better, but . . . ," he paused.

"But what?"

"But Mom, what about the milkweed?"

"What do you mean?"

"Mr. Garcia said we have to get rid of it to save Dune. He already sprayed part of his yard and plans to spray the rest plus our yard on Friday. He also said the county will be mowing the roadsides Friday, and that's where most of the milkweed grows. What about the monarchs?"

"Hmmm," she thought for a moment. "If they aren't harming Dune, maybe we don't need to get rid of them."

"But we don't know for sure they aren't harming Dune, and anyway, Mr. Garcia was getting rid of them because he said they're weeds."

"I don't remember seeing any milkweeds that were actually weeds."

"Then why are they called milk*weeds*?" asked Tai.

"The name confuses a lot of people. Plants are only weeds if they are where they aren't meant to be. I'm pretty sure I only saw native milkweeds around your pasture and roadside, but I'll go back out and look again to be sure.

"Also, even if there are milkweeds we need to keep away from Dune, we won't need chemicals to kill them. We can fence them off or pull them by hand." She paused to think before continuing. "With my botany knowledge and Stephanie's veterinary skills, we should be able to put our heads together and figure out what to do. How about if I talk to her about it when we call in the morning?"

“Thanks, Mom,” Tai smiled. “See you in the morning.”

“See you in the morning, Taiyo-kun. Sweet dreams.”

10

As Tai and his mother slept, Dana remained in her green chrysalis. She continued to hang upside-down from her silk attachment, silently waiting and rocking gently in the breeze.

11

On Wednesday morning, Dune showed a lot of improvement.

"Let's call Stephanie so you can give her an update on Dune," Tai's mom said. "Then she and I can also discuss the milkweeds." She dialed the phone and handed it to Tai.

"Hello, Tai?" answered Stephanie.

"Yes, it's me," Tai replied, his voice strong and upbeat. "Dune is doing better. My lucky penny is working! Oh, and your advice probably helped, too," Tai teased somewhat awkwardly.

"That's great news!"

"Now, we need your help with something else," said Tai. "We need to know what to do about the milkweeds. My mom said she would talk to you about it. Even though my mom works as a dentist, she's also a really good botanist and knows a ton about plants. She said since she knows about plants and you know about horses, maybe you two could figure it out."

"We sure will give it a try," said Stephanie.

"Um . . . thank you for the help," Tai added before handing the phone to his mom.

Tai listened while his mom and Stephanie had a long discussion—mostly about milkweeds—but also ranging into other subjects. It was filled with laughter and pauses to consult the Internet.

Finally, his mother hung up the phone and looked over at Tai, who was still watching her. "We can save the milkweeds without hurting Dune," she said with a smile.

"All of them?"

"All of them."

"And they won't hurt Dune?"

"They won't hurt him. Milkweeds taste bitter. Dune lives on a healthy pasture with plenty of good-tasting, healthy grass and forbs. There's no reason for him to eat the milkweed. Also, most of the milkweeds here have nice wide leaves and are easy for Dune to see and avoid."

Tai took a deep breath and let it out slowly. "What a relief." Then he paused a minute to think. "But what do you mean by 'most'? Are there others that don't have nice wide leaves?"

"Yes. There are some narrow-leaf milkweeds. They are more toxic than the other milkweeds and harder for Dune to avoid. Stephanie doesn't think Dune will eat them, and even if he did, it would take a lot to make him sick, but if it makes you less worried, she said we can fence them off."

"Got it. But what are you going to do to keep Mr. Garcia from spraying this Friday?" asked Tai earnestly.

"What am *I* going to do? Aren't you, Izzy, and Brooke part of the Nature Club? Isn't the Nature Club supposed to learn about nature and take action to help it?"

"Well, yeah," agreed Tai. "And, actually, Izzy's little brother, Zack, is sometimes in it, too. And Izzy's pen pal, Miguel, sends us advice from Nicaragua."

"Well, all right then. What is the *Nature Club* going to do?" she asked, smiling. "The way I see it, you kids have two tasks. First, go next door and talk to Mr. Garcia about why you want to keep the milkweed. Tell him it's not a weed, it won't hurt Dune, and you don't want chemicals sprayed on your pasture. Tell him that, to be sure, you will fence off the narrow-leaf milkweed.

"Second, call the county and ask them not to cut back the roadsides, in order to protect the milkweed. Since it's already Wednesday afternoon and both Mr. Garcia and the county plan to take action Friday, I suggest you get moving."

12

At first, Tai stood with his mouth open. *Go to Mr. Garcia's house?* he thought. *I can't go there, that guy is intimidating.* But then he thought, *she didn't say "Tai," she said, "the Nature Club," which means Brooke, Izzy, and even Zack have to come with me.* Tai finally closed his mouth and said, "No problem." He then flashed a nervous smile at his mom and got on the phone.

First, Tai called Izzy and Zack, and then he called Brooke. They decided to meet at Tai's house in half an hour. When they arrived, Tai had already pulled some wire fencing out of the shed to enclose the two patches of narrow-leaf milkweed. With the four of them working together, it only took a half hour.

Then they sat on Tai's front porch to work out a strategy for what to do next. Approaching Mr.

Garcia was by far the hardest task, so they considered ways to talk to him without really talking to him. Izzy suggested they write a letter, Brooke said they could call him anonymously, and Tai proposed sneaking into Mr. Garcia's yard and hiding his chemicals.

When they couldn't agree, Tai said, "Izzy, you're the president of the Nature Club—how about you make the decision?"

"I think we need to go to his house and talk to him in person," Izzy said.

"Are you sure you can do that?" Tai asked, knowing Izzy was the shyest of all of them.

"Izzy won't be doing it," Brooke said. "Tai, *you* need to do the talking. You are the one who knows him, and Dune is your horse. But we'll go with you."

"Right," Izzy agreed. "After that, calling the county will be easy. Brooke can do that. She can talk to anyone."

"Okay, I'll do that," Brooke agreed immediately. "Also, my dad knows people at the county office and can help me talk to the right person."

"Okay then," Tai said, clenching his teeth. "I'll do it. I'm not scared of Mr. Garcia. I'll go over there right now."

Izzy and Brooke looked at each other with raised eyebrows. "Okay then, let's go," Brooke challenged.

Tai stood up straight, hoping the others couldn't hear the thumping of his heart, and walked directly over to Mr. Garcia's house. When they got to the porch, they stopped and scanned the house, with Tai hoping there would be no sign of anyone home. Unfortunately for him, the living room light was on, and they could see the shape of a person sitting on the couch next to a vase of flowers.

"Well? What are you waiting for, Mr. 'I'm not scared'? Knock on the door," Brooke directed.

Tai lifted his hand, paused, and then gave the door two solid knocks.

The three of them stood together, anxiously

listening for footsteps. At first, they heard none, so they quickly turned to leave, but just as suddenly, someone clomped up, the door opened, and Mr. Garcia appeared. He was so tall he towered over them. He was wearing a blood-stained apron and held a butcher knife in his right hand. All three kids gasped and stood frozen.

As Mr. Garcia lowered his eyes to meet theirs, the kids stood absolutely quiet, each one staring at either Mr. Garcia or his knife. Then, suddenly, from the room behind Mr. Garcia, someone coughed, making Izzy scream. Izzy's scream in turn made Brooke break into a nervous fit of giggles.

"Harold, who's at the door?" a woman's voice called from inside.

"It's Tai from next door, with some girls," he called back. Mr. Garcia then realized he was still holding a knife and had scared the girl who had screamed. "Oh, I'm sorry, I was just carving up a dead body," he said while making a scary face.

Izzy stepped back and nearly fell off the porch,

a look of horror on her face.

"Pay no attention to Harold," said the woman, finally coming into view as she rolled up in a wheelchair. "He's harmless. He was cutting up a raspberry pie and couldn't find a smaller knife. Would you kids like a piece?"

"I love pie," replied Brooke, while Tai and Izzy tried to recover from their shock over the greeting. "We came with Tai so he could talk to Mr. Garcia about the milkweed plants."

"The weeds? Oh, yes, Harold's been fixated on them ever since I had my accident. Do you know about it?"

All three kids silently shook their heads.

"Three years ago, I was driving home from work when a bear ran across the road, causing another car to swerve and run into my car. I broke my spine and have been in this chair ever since. Harold's been so sweet, taking care of me, always putting wildflowers in a vase in our window, and lobbying to get the county to trim the road edges to make another accident less likely."

"And don't forget making pies," Harold added.

"He does make a darn good pie," the woman confided to the kids.

"I'm . . . I'm so sorry about your accident," stuttered Izzy.

"Oh, that's sweet of you. But don't worry about me. I'll be fine. We're just trying to make sure it doesn't happen to anyone else."

"Why would trimming the weeds make another accident less likely?" asked Brooke.

"Because when there are fewer plants along the side of the road for animals to hide in, they stay farther from the road. Also, it's easier to see them when everything is trimmed, so it's less likely cars will hit them—or have to swerve to avoid hitting them."

"I thought you just wanted to get rid of the milkweeds because you don't like weeds—and to protect Dune," Tai said. "I didn't know there was another reason," he added quietly, glancing at Mrs. Garcia.

"Well, you're right, I don't want Dune

poisoned," Mr. Garcia said. "For me, the biggest reason to get rid of milkweed—and all other tall roadside plants—is to make the roads safer. I don't even know for sure which are actually weeds—my wife is the nature lover in the family. To me, they all look like plants, and when I want them gone, I call them weeds."

"That's true," Mrs. Garcia chimed in. "And I'm especially crazy for the *mariposas*."

"The what?" Brooke asked.

"*Mariposa* is Spanish for 'butterfly'," Mrs. Garcia explained.

"Us, too!" exclaimed Brooke. "We all love mariposas! That's why we want to save the milkweed plants."

"You kids must come in and tell us what you're talking about over some pie," Mrs. Garcia said. "I won't take no for an answer."

Mr. Garcia brought a phone to Tai, who wanted to call his dad first to get permission. Mr. and Mrs. Garcia then made them feel comfortable around the kitchen table, where they enjoyed lemonade and pie. Finally, the kids started talking. They explained why monarchs need milkweeds and how they already had fenced off the two small patches of narrow-leaf milkweeds to keep Dune from eating them. When they were done, Mrs. Garcia said, “Harold, these kids are right. We need to save those milkweeds.”

“If these kids can convince the county to avoid cutting the milkweeds while still cutting all the other weeds, then I can support it. But only if they still cut the other weeds,” said Mr. Garcia with the hint of a smile. But then his face stiffened, and he added, “We cannot let another accident happen.”

When the kids left, it was past five o’clock—too late for Brooke to call the county, but she promised to ask her dad for help the next day.

Feeling optimistic, Tai went straight to Dune to check on him. Dune had so much more energy than he’d had in previous days that Tai thought briefly about taking him to the arena for a practice session. Then he thought back to Stephanie’s advice, which was to let Dune fully recover. Tai knew she was right, even if it meant missing the race on Saturday.

He sighed, and instead of heading to the arena for a practice, he just walked with Dune around the pasture. Although he was disappointed about missing the rodeo, he was even more relieved and grateful Dune was going to be okay.

13

The following morning, Brooke asked her dad how to contact the county. Always ready to help with a good cause, her dad, Mr. Clark, called right when the office opened. After some confusion, he found out that the person to talk to was named Janet Helling, and soon he was connected to her.

"County road maintenance, Janet speaking," she said.

"Terrific," said Mr. Clark. "I'm going to turn the phone over to my daughter, Brooke. She's calling on behalf of a group called the Nature Club because she has some questions for you."

Brooke smiled and took the phone. "Hello, this is Brooke with the Nature Club."

"The Nature Club. Why does that sound familiar?" asked Janet.

"We organized the garbage pickup at Green

County Park and got into the newspaper for it!"

"Ah, yes. That was a terrific event! How can I help you?"

Brooke eagerly explained about how the Nature Club wanted to save milkweeds but were worried a lot of milkweeds would be lost when the county did its roadside clearing on Friday. She said they understood why roadside clearing was important, but so were monarchs.

Janet listened carefully and then said, "Well, you're talking to the right person. I'm the one who does the clearing, and you're right, it is scheduled for Friday," she paused. "Do you have a plan for how to save the milkweeds that allows for the trimming of the roads?"

"We, uh, we don't actually have a plan yet—but we know we want to help," Brooke answered brightly.

"My mother always said, 'enthusiasm will get you everywhere,' and I believe that," said Janet. "A few years ago, I found out there were birds that nested in plants I was cutting, so now I wait until they can fly before I do the cutting. Let's think and see if we can find a solution to this, too."

After talking through their shared goals and considering possible solutions, Janet and Brooke came up with a plan. The kids would meet up with Janet on Friday. They would mark the milkweed plants with orange flagging so Janet could see and avoid cutting them.

Brooke hung up the phone and called Izzy and Tai with the news. She reminded Izzy to bring her little brother, Zack, so they could work in two teams of two. She also asked them to wear the matching Nature Club T-shirts Mr. Clark had made for them a few weeks earlier.

Friday morning, the kids showed up early, all wearing boots, jeans, and their Nature Club T-shirts. Brooke's dad also showed up to help.

Janet arrived soon after with a big mower truck and a second worker named Zane. They parked the truck to walk over to meet the kids and shake Mr. Clark's hand.

"Thanks for working with us," said Mr. Clark.

"I'm sure you're busy, and we appreciate your modifying your work to help the monarchs."

"Hey, if these kids have a good idea *and* are willing to put in an honest day's work instead of sitting in front of a screen, I'm happy to work with them," said Janet.

"Amen to that," added Zane. "And nice to meet you, Mr. Clark."

"Likewise," Mr. Clark said.

"You got it," said Zane. "Should we get started?" he asked Janet.

"Yes," she answered and then turned to address the whole group. "I'm going to have you kids work in two groups to mark the milkweeds with orange flags. One group will work with Mr. Clark to mark the plants with flagging ahead of the mower, and the other group will work with Zane to remove the flagging behind the mower. I'll drive the mower. Did you bring your own gloves and orange vests?"

"We did," Brooke answered for the group.

"Great," said Janet. "Zane will give you a safety

talk, and then we'll get started."

The day was hot and the mosquitos were biting, but the group worked steadily right up until five o'clock. At five, Janet pulled over and turned off the mower. "Great work, team. We can call it a day."

"What about the other roadsides?" asked Brooke.

"And the parking lot at Green County Park?" Izzy added.

"I checked out the other roadsides, and there aren't many milkweed plants. I'm not sure about the parking lot. Do you know?"

"The edge of the parking area is loaded with milkweed," Tai piped in.

"Okay. I'll just skip mowing it this year. There's no road hazard there, so it isn't really necessary."

"Awesome!" said Brooke.

"No worries. I'm behind anyway and don't really have time for it."

"Did we slow you way down?" asked Izzy.

"You know, I thought you would, but nope. I'm

behind because of rainy days—not because of the little time it took to avoid the milkweeds. In fact, I'll make avoiding milkweeds part of the program."

"Double awesome!" Tai cheered. "Hey, I don't know about the rest of you, but I need to get home to Dune." Everyone agreed it was time to get home for dinner. Tai, anxious to see Dune, jumped on his bike and quickly pedaled off.

When he got home, he was surprised to find his mother helping Stephanie give Dune a thorough exam out in the pasture. As he walked up to join them, he could see they were laughing and having fun. It just seemed so . . . unexpected. He took a deep breath and walked right up. "Taiyo-kun!" greeted his mother.

"Hi, Tai," added Stephanie. "Dune is doing really well. I'm amazed at his quick recovery. You've taken very good care of him."

"Does that mean we can still—"

"Nope," said Stephanie, cutting him off. "Dune is doing great, but he needs another two weeks of rest and can't race tomorrow. But—"

"But," his mother took over, "the rodeo was postponed by two weeks anyway because there was a small fire in the bleachers. No one was hurt, but they need time to make repairs."

"You're kidding," said Tai, wide-eyed. "Dune and I will get to race? Woohoo!" he hollered. "Only . . . ," he paused and looked at his mother, "you won't be there."

"Actually, I will. I decided to stay longer to watch you . . . *and* . . . to look for a place to live. Chase is going to fly in the weekend of the rodeo to meet you and check out the town."

"Really?"

"Really. One of the reasons I became a dentist was so I could live anywhere, and I want to live near you. This town is as good as any, and Chase is willing to give it a try."

Tai whooped again and jumped into his mother's arms. They celebrated for so long that finally even Stephanie joined in. When they broke apart, Tai looked between the two women and asked, “Can this really work?”

“Absolutely,” said Stephanie, smiling at Tai’s mother.

As they talked, Tai’s dad walked over and asked, “What’s so exciting over here?”

“We told him,” his mother said.

“Everything?” he asked.

“Yes. We told him about Dune getting better, the rodeo being postponed, and my moving here. I think he liked the news,” she said, pointing to Tai, who was standing next to her with a giant grin on his face.

“Dad,” Tai said, his voice shaking, “this is the best news ever!”

“Well then,” his dad said, putting his arm around Tai. “Let’s not just stand around. We need to celebrate. Come on team. I made a great dinner and have all the fixings for ice cream sundaes for dessert.”

The group walked to the house for what would be the first of many celebrations together. Over dinner, they came up with a plan for Tai to nurse

Dune back to full health for another week, and then to spend a week training with him at the arena: slowly at first and increasing until he was ready by competition time.

14

Over the next two weeks, as Dune transformed back to good health, an even more miraculous transformation happened in the Garcias' yard. There, on the last live milkweed that stood next to a row of dead milkweed plants, Dana's chrysalis—once an emerald green—became translucent.

It was so clear, you could see Dana right through it. She now had orange and black coloring, for the yellow, black, and green caterpillar she once was had transformed into a monarch butterfly, and she was ready to emerge.

Then, very late in the day on a Friday, as Tai brushed Dune on the other side of the fence, Dana's clear chrysalis broke open and she emerged as an adult butterfly with small, brightly colored wings. At first, she hardly moved as she hung on tightly to the end of the torn chrysalis. But then, over the next hour, her wings grew bigger and bigger until they expanded to their full size. They were a stunning reddish-orange, with striking black edges, white dots, and a network of black lines within.

Now, fully transformed, Dana searched for nectar. She found nectar in a range of plants but still favored the milkweed. To harvest a milkweed's nectar, she stood unsteadily on the petals of a cluster of pink milkweed flowers. Dana then slowly flapped her wings up and down while using her proboscis—a long, straw-like tongue—to drink the nectar within each flower.

As she worked her way through the flowers, one of her feet slipped into a slit in the flower. She pulled her foot out, not noticing that a pollen sac was now stuck to her foot, and she continued to feed on nectar. She also didn't take any notice of a bee that also was feeding on the nectar of the same milkweed plant.

When Dana flew to another milkweed plant to feed, the pollen sac stuck to her foot rubbed off onto the second plant. As a result, the flowers on the second plant were pollinated and from them, large seed pods would emerge at the end of summer. Then in early fall, the pods would split open and release their seeds to the wind.

Soon, Dana would rest from feeding and begin to lay her own eggs, thus ensuring there would be a generation of monarchs able to make the long journey to their wintering grounds.

15

The next day was rodeo day. The two-week delay had given Dune time to rest, recover, and even spend a few days training with Tai. He wasn't at his best, but he was still strong. Tai told his friends he just wanted to compete, but, secretly, he desperately wanted to place in the top three spots so he could walk away with a trophy.

Tai and his dad left for the rodeo grounds early, pulling the horse trailer with Dune inside. It was a one-hour drive, during which they mostly sat in silence. Tai was lost in thought, and his dad was simply enjoying the drive and Tai's company.

When they arrived, they first stopped at the registration table, where they learned there would be only ten racers in Tai's age group—fewer than Tai had raced in Nebraska. Scanning the list of names, Tai found that one of the other racers would be riding Golden Moon—the horse that likely had gotten Dune sick back at his local arena. Otherwise, none of the names looked familiar.

Tai and his dad then took Dune to his assigned stall. Dune had so much trust in Tai that when Tai led the horse in, he took to it easily. Three stalls down, Tai found Golden Moon. The rider was nowhere to be found, so Tai stood and checked out the horse. As he did, another rider joined him, saying, "I hear this is a really fast horse. She's expected to be the winner."

"No kidding? I've seen this horse at my local arena, but I've never seen her run."

"Golden Moon used to always come in at under fifteen and a half seconds with her last owner," the boy said.

"*Under* fifteen and a half seconds? I don't have a chance," Tai said, his eyes wide.

"Right, but that was with her last owner. It's her new owner who'll be riding today."

"What happened to her old owner?" Tai asked.

"I think her name was Emily. Her family moved to North Carolina and couldn't take her horse with them."

"Wow. That's sad. I almost had to leave my horse when I moved, but then my dad found a house with a pasture. I didn't realize how lucky I was," Tai smiled. "What horse are you racing on?"

"I'm on Starry Sky. She's the cinnamon-brown quarter horse in that last stall," he said. "My name's Alden. This is my first real race. I'm nervous I'm going to mess up," he admitted.

"Hey, Alden. I'm Tai. Don't worry. Once you get moving, you won't think of anything except gettin' around those barrels."

"I hope. Well, I'm going to get back to her. Good luck," called Alden, already turning to get back to his horse.

"You, too," Tai said, feeling anxious to get back to Dune.

Tai and his dad stayed with Dune through the morning, with Tai leaving only once to check on Alden and take a look at Alden's horse, Starry Sky.

Tai was feeling less confident about winning a trophy after learning about Golden Moon's times and needed a distraction. Tai and Dune's fastest run was 15.9 seconds, but Dune was still recovering. Tai also kept looking over at Golden Moon to see if her rider was there, but the horse was on her own the entire morning.

For lunch, Tai and his dad walked out to the concessions area to get some food. While they were out, they also stopped in the stands to say hello to their friends and family. There was a huge crowd there to support Tai and Dune. Brooke had come with her parents. Izzy had come with Zack and her baby brother, her mother, and her mother's boyfriend, Cody. Tai's mom and her boyfriend, Chase, had driven in with Stephanie.

The Garcias had even come to watch. Since there was a special section of the stands set up to accommodate wheelchairs, the whole group sat there to be together. "Your son sure throws a great party!" Mr. Garcia said to Mr. Davis.

"This is a lot of fun," Stephanie added. "Out of

Tai's whole cheering section, Suki is the only one who's been to a rodeo before, so we're learning a lot and having a great time. The kids especially love the clowns, and get this: Izzy's little brother, Zack competed in the stick horse competition."

"He did what?" Mr. Davis asked.

"The stick horse competition. They had kids ages five and six come out and race on stick horses—you know, the long sticks with the stuffed horse heads at the top? He came in second to last. It was so funny."

"Oh, right!" Mr. Davis said. "Tai used to join the stick horse race when he was little."

"No kidding. I don't even remember," Tai said. "I wish I could've seen Zack in it!"

"Me too," Mr. Davis said. Then he turned to the others. "The barrel racing is right after lunch. Keep your fingers crossed for Tai!"

"We will!" Stephanie said.

"Tai, we're all rooting for you—and Dune," Izzy said.

"You've got this!" Brooke added.

"I'll give it my best shot," Tai said. "It sure helps to have a great partner like Dune."

After everyone gave Tai words of support, he and his dad went back to be with Dune. As Tai got increasingly nervous, the time seemed to go more and more slowly. Finally, at one o'clock, it was time for the race. The races went by age group, from youngest to oldest, with Tai's group going third. As the first two groups raced, Tai could feel a knot form in his stomach. He looked around and waved to Alden, who waved back.

He also saw Golden Moon's rider had finally arrived and gotten ready. Tai knew from her long braids that she was the same girl he'd seen with Golden Moon at his local arena, so he waved, but she didn't wave back. That normally would have bothered Tai, but today he was too focused on Dune.

In barrel racing—an event requiring speed, technique, and agility—you ride your horse in a cloverleaf pattern around three equally spaced barrels. The rider with the fastest time wins. To be fast, you have to have perfect communication with your horse, which requires teamwork, practice, and concentration.

After the second group finished, a tractor drove out to smooth the dirt on the race course. As soon as it was clear, Tai's group got started. He was the tenth and final racer. As he waited with Dune at the edge of the arena, he could feel the pounding of his heart and worried about the competition. Although most racers were clocking in at sixteen seconds or more, one clocked in at 15.6 seconds and another at 15.7 seconds—faster than Tai and Dune's best.

The ninth racer was the girl with the long braids riding on Golden Moon. When it was their turn, they shot out into the arena. They had amazing speed. But when they got to the first barrel, they had to slow. The rider didn't seem to know her horse well enough to get her around the barrel while keeping their momentum. The same was true for all three barrels. As fast as Golden Moon ran, it wasn't fast enough to make up for their lack of teamwork, and they came in at exactly 15.9 seconds.

While it was much slower than Golden Moon's record, it was the same as Tai and Dune's fastest—when Dune was at his healthiest. Tai looked down at Dune and said, "Let's not worry about the others. This is our last competition together before you retire. Let's just have fun and do our best—as a team." Then Tai looked up and took a deep breath. They were ready.

The moment Tai signaled Dune to start, Dune raced into the arena at top speed and easily rounded the first barrel. Tai was so focused on Dune, he didn't hear the thunderous cheers from his friends in the stands. It felt like he and Dune were moving as one as they rounded the second and the third barrels, and in no time, they raced toward the finish.

With dust flying and his heart pounding, Tai knew they had done well. It turned out they had done better than well—they had set a personal record of 15.8 seconds, putting them solidly into third place. Tai and Dune would stand on the podium and take home a trophy after all!

16

On Sunday afternoon, the group gathered for a celebratory barbecue at Tai's house. Brooke's dad made his famous barbecue sauce, Izzy baked brownies, Mrs. Clark brought a watermelon, and Mr. Garcia made two homemade pies.

Before they sat down to eat, Tai brought Dune over to the group and asked his dad to get everyone's attention.

"Everyone. Hey, everyone!" his father shouted. When the group gathered, he said, "We are celebrating Tai and Dune's third-place win yesterday, but we're also celebrating Dune's retirement. Tai, would you like to say something?"

Tai turned to Dune and said out loud, his eyes wet with tears, "Dune. You're the best horse and the best friend I could ever want. We sure make a great team." At that, he placed a wreath of wildflowers around Dune's neck and gave him a fresh bale of sweet hay while everyone clapped and cheered.

Then Dustin and Suki stood together in front of the group. Suki said, "Taiyo-kun, I couldn't be prouder of you—and of Dune. Not because you won, but because you showed us all how great teamwork is done."

"But also," added Dustin, "we sure are proud of your win. Let's all give a cheer to Green County barrel racing champions Tai and Dune!"

"Hooray!" everyone cheered.

"And if I may add," said Mr. Garcia, causing the whole group to quiet down and listen, "I would like to make a toast." Everyone raised their glasses, and he said, "Here's to Tai and the Nature Club, for teaching me about the special relationship between monarchs and these beautiful, *native* plants we call milkweeds!"

"Hooray!" everyone cheered again.

"Aw, thanks, everyone," gushed Tai. "Mr.

Garcia reminded me, I think the Nature Club has a toast, too. Izzy, you're the club president. Can you start it?"

"Um . . . yes. Okay," answered Izzy awkwardly. "Let's all raise our glasses to nature."

"And milkweeds!" added Tai.

"And monarchs!" cheered Brooke.

And the group yelled out a final "Hooray!"

"Okay, team," called Stephanie, "it's time to eat." As the group helped each other find seats, Tai watched his mother and Chase set the table while Stephanie and his father organized the food.

Taking a deep breath, he realized that maybe each of his parents had found a better match and that, maybe, everything would turn out okay. Brooke, who was standing next to Tai and must have been watching the same thing, said, "It's almost like you now have four parents. I wonder how many presents you'll get on your birthday this year?"

"Good question!" he said.

"What will you do now that you're done with barrel racing?" Izzy asked.

"You know what?" Tai said. "I think I'm going to concentrate on the Nature Club because when you have a good team, you should stick with it!"

Izzy, Brooke, and Zack all smiled broadly and gave Tai a group hug.

Suddenly, Mr. Garcia shouted, "Look at that beautiful butterfly," pointing to an orange and black butterfly that had just fluttered into the Davises' pasture from his own yard.

Everyone stopped what they were doing to take a look. "Mr. Garcia, that's one of the monarchs!" Tai said, no longer afraid of his neighbor.

The butterfly flew right over to them and landed on Mr. Garcia's head. "Finally, I can get a good look at the two things I love most at the very same time!" his wife said. Everyone laughed.

As the group watched, the monarch sailed off into the pasture and landed on a large, healthy milkweed to lay its eggs.

Notes on Monarchs

by Tai Davis

Monarch butterflies are also known as *Danaus plexippus* in Latin. They are bright orange, have a network of black veins, and have a black border with white spots. Monarchs are big butterflies with wings that measure up to four inches across but each one weighs less than my lucky penny.

They live in North, Central, and South America; Australia; some Pacific Islands;

India; and Western Europe.

North American monarchs migrate up to three thousand miles each year! They spend summers in Canada or the United States and winters in Southern California or Central Mexico. One butterfly makes the entire trip south, but it takes a bunch of generations for monarchs to return north. Even with no single butterfly making the entire trip north, the butterflies arrive at the same breeding and wintering grounds every year!

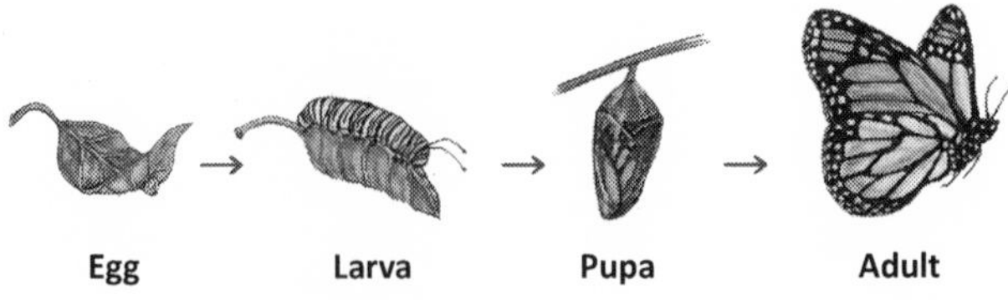

Like all butterflies, monarchs go through metamorphosis. During it,

monarchs have a one-of-a-kind relationship with milkweed plants. Monarchs lay their eggs only on milkweed plants, and when the larvae emerge as green, black, and white striped caterpillars, they feed only on milkweed plants.

Milkweed

As caterpillars, they then go through five growth periods called "instars" and then they're ready to change into butterflies. As butterflies, monarchs are less picky—they get nectar from a bunch of different plants.

The final larval instar spins silk to attach itself to the underside of a milkweed plant, sheds its skin, and forms a *pupa*, or chrysalis. Inside, the butterfly forms. When it comes out, it sits for a few hours to dry out its wings. Then it flies off to find nectar and, if its female, lay eggs.

The cool thing about the monarch-milkweed partnership is that the milkweed has a type of poison the monarchs incorporate into their own bodies. When a predator tries to eat a monarch and tastes the poison, it becomes sick and starts to avoid eating monarchs. The poison works so well that predators also avoid another butterfly, the viceroy, just because it looks like a monarch.

***

To protect monarchs and other butterflies:

- Protect and plant native plants, especially milkweed plants and plants that provide nectar to butterflies.
- Have a chemical-free garden to not poison butterflies or other wildlife.
- Keep cats indoors and dogs on leashes so they don't kill butterflies.
- Reduce, reuse, recycle, and pick up litter to protect the butterflies' habitat.
- Never transfer and release butterflies into new locations to avoid spreading diseases among different groups of butterflies.

Questions to Consider:

1. Tai has a close partnership with his horse, Dune. What makes it special?

2. How does Tai deal with the disappointment of possibly not getting to ride in the rodeo? How do you deal with disappointment?

3. What is unique about the monarch butterfly's migration?

4. In what ways do monarch butterflies depend on milkweed plants?

5. What did Tai learn that prepared him to accept his parents' divorce?

6. What are some ways you can protect monarch butterflies?

Join the Nature Club for more adventures!

www.natureclubbooks.com

Read on for a peek at Book 3 . . .

The Everywhere Bear
Chapter 1

Brooke laughed as she jumped from log to log, her dark, curly hair bouncing as she went. She wanted to reach the edge of the creek without touching the ground, which was muddy from last night's rain. For some reason, the logs looked blurry to her, so each time she jumped, she had to rely on a bit of luck. It was working well until her last jump—when she landed on something slippery and fell on her butt in the muck. "Gross," she groaned, realizing she had slid right through a pile of animal poop.

Brooke stood up and looked down at her mud-stained purple shorts. As she examined the mess, she noticed a set of tracks in the mud. Squinting to look at them, she first thought they were from a human. There were tracks that looked like they were made from human hands, and others that looked like they were made from human feet. Then she bent over to study them and saw that, on the tracks of the feet, the toes were all long and the big one pointed outward.

So it couldn't be a human, Brooke thought. *But what are they from? What walks on all fours and has big toes that look more like thumbs?* She considered it for a bit and finally snapped her fingers. *They must be from a monkey,* she thought.

At that moment, her best friends, Izzy and Tai, walked up and with a simple, "Hi Brooke," made her jump.

"Oh, hi," she replied while continuing to study the tracks.

"What are you looking at, and why are you so muddy?" Izzy asked, looking at the mud splattered all over Brooke's legs. "You even have mud up on your purple headband."

"Hey, ignore the mud for a second. I found some monkey tracks over here," Brooke replied. Izzy and Tai glanced at each other and burst out laughing.

"You found *what*?" Izzy asked while eyeing Tai with a smile.

"You heard her," grinned Tai, tipping his tan cowboy hat toward the tracks. "She found tracks from the little-known American monkey."

"Brooke, there are no monkeys in the United States. Unless one escaped from a zoo," Izzy said between giggles.

Brooke frowned and straightened up. "You're just jealous you didn't find them," she said.

"Right," Tai said. "Let's take a look." Tai and Izzy surrounded Brooke to look at the tracks.

"They do look like monkey tracks," Izzy observed.

Tai gave Izzy a sideways glance. "Now I think you're both crazy," he said.

"Well then, what are they from?" Brooke challenged.

"I don't know," Tai replied.

"Let's find out," Izzy suggested. "I'll go get the mammal track guidebook and be right back." Then she ran off toward the house her family was renting for the summer, which was right near Green County Park.

While Izzy was gone, Tai asked, "How did you come up with a monkey?"

"I'll tell you if you promise to stop laughing," Brooke responded with her hands on her hips.

"I promise to stop laughing," Tai said, trying to keep a straight face.

"Okay. Since the tracks look human, but the big toe looks more like a thumb, they have to be from a monkey," Brooke explained.

"I know how we can find out for sure," Izzy said after returning with a ruler, a camera, and her guidebook on local animals' tracks.

"Let's measure the tracks and compare them with what the book shows," Izzy said.

"And then," Tai added with a smile, "we'll see if we still come up with a monkey."

Brooke rolled her eyes and pulled a half-eaten Astro Bar out of her pocket.

"Hey! Next time, bring some of those bars for us, too," Tai said.

"I got a box of these candy bars last week from a neighbor and I can't stop eating them. They are delicious. I'd give you one—but they are only for monkey trackers."

"Oh, come on," Tai pleaded. "I'll track a whole troupe of monkeys with you."

"Too late. It was my last one," Brooke smiled and popped the last piece into her mouth.

"Hey, chocolate lovers. Are you ready to get to work?" Izzy asked.

"Sure thing, President Izzy," Tai joked. Izzy, who was the president of their Nature Club despite her shy personality, blushed and handed him the measuring tape. Then she pulled her straight brown hair into her standard ponytail to get started.

Together, they measured the length and width of each print and the length and width of the distance between the prints. They also took note of the gait—the pattern of steps and how they fell in relation to each other.

Tai then took a few photos while Izzy flipped through the book. Brooke tried to follow along by peering over Izzy's shoulder, but the words on the pages looked blurry from where she stood.

“Let’s see,” Izzy said as she flipped through the book. “The larger tracks are almost four inches long, so we can rule out all the little critters, like mice, squirrels, and chipmunks.

“And there are a bunch of things it obviously isn’t—like a deer or a rabbit or a coyote.

“It looks kind of like an opossum,” she continued, “but the tracks are larger, and their gait is different. And it looks kind of like a river otter, but it’s—”

“Stop telling us what it isn’t. Just tell us what it is,” Brooke pleaded.

Izzy looked at Brooke crossly for a moment and then turned back to flipping through the book. Finally, she yelled, “Aha! There’s your monkey!”

Tai leaned over Izzy to look at the book. “You’re right, Izzy. The tracks match.” Pointing to some text under the photo of the track, he added, “Even the habitat is right. It says, ‘Raccoon tracks are often found near water.’”

"Are you sure?" Brooke asked.

"Sorry, Brooke. It's lookin' like today's not the day you become famous," Tai said. "But raccoons are cool, too. Right?"

"Right," Brooke sighed.

"Hey, look," Izzy added, "on the next page there's a picture of raccoon scat." Noticing Brooke's confused look, Izzy explained, "You know, poop. Scat is animal poop. If we had some scat, we could be even more sure we're right."

Brooke sighed. "Well, actually, we might," she said, running her fingers through her thick, curly, dark hair.

"Where?" Izzy asked.

"On top of that log right there," Brooke said, pointing. "I accidentally stepped in it when I jumped on the log. I slid through it and fell in the mud." She turned around and showed her friends the big muddy spot on the back of her shorts.

Tai and Izzy burst into another round of laughter as they made their way to the log to examine what was left of the scat. Although it was squished, it did look like the scat in the picture.

Brooke now also laughed. “I guess a monkey was a bit of a stretch for this habitat.”

“Let’s see if we can figure out what the raccoon was doing,” Izzy suggested.

“Great idea,” Tai said. He backed up to look at the entire set of tracks. “Watch where you walk,” he added, careful to not step on the prints.

From a bit of a distance, it was easier to investigate where the tracks came from and where they went. It looked as if the raccoon had entered the beach from the nearby bushes, walked straight to the water, and then walked back to the bushes. From there, the tracks disappeared.

Brooke called to Izzy. “Can you read what raccoons do in water?”

Izzy, who was still looking at the tracks, said, “Can you do it? The book is in your backpack. I stuck it in there so it wouldn’t get muddy.” After a dramatic pause, she added, “Not that there was much room in your bag with all the Astro Bar wrappers in there."

Brooke mumbled something about not cleaning out her backpack for a while and then went to retrieve the book. She opened it and found the raccoon page, but the words looked blurry and she could barely make them out. Handing the book to Izzy, she said, "Come on, you're the bookworm. You read it."

Izzy stood up and looked at Brooke sideways, but then she took the book and scanned the page. "Raccoons are omnivores and will eat almost anything that comes their way," she read. "If they're near water, they will wet their food before eating it."

"Well, isn't that polite of them?" Brooke observed.

"Actually," Izzy responded, "they don't wet their food to wash it. It says here they wet it 'to increase the sensitivity of their paws to feel and identify their food.'"

With that mystery solved, the kids hung out at the creek and sketched in their journals until Izzy said, “I’d better go get my little brother, Zack, from my Grandma Pearl’s house.”

“I’d better get going, too,” Brooke said. “I told my dad I’d help make dinner.”

“Ditto,” Tai said. “I want to get home and ride my horse, Dune, before dark.”

As always since forming the Nature Club, the friends spent time picking up trash before leaving. They had sponsored a community trash pickup day right there at Green County Park just the month before, so it should have been clean. But it was a mess! Strangely, the biggest mess came from behind the bush, the same spot where the raccoon tracks emerged.

“That poor raccoon is hanging out in a mess,” Izzy observed.

“A gross mess,” Brooke agreed. “Hey, look,” she said, pointing to an Astro Bar wrapper in the bush. “At least the litterbug has good taste in candy bars.”

“Too bad someone already ate that one, too,” Tai groaned. “It wasn’t you, was it?”

“Are you accusing me of littering?” Brooke asked, her eyes wide open.

“Maybe . . . .” Tai looked at Brooke’s horrified expression. “Oops. I guess not. Sorry.”

“Grrrrr!” Brooke replied.

“Okay, you two, we’re all friends here. Let’s get to work,” Izzy said. The three of them worked until the bulk of the mess was bagged up and stuffed into the park’s dumpster. Then the friends spent some time making notes about what they saw and sketching the tracks in their journals before parting for the evening. Tai retrieved his bike to pedal home while Brooke and Izzy left together. After they said goodbye at Izzy’s house, Brooke continued to the end of the road where she lived with her mom and dad.

to be continued . . .

Acknowledgments

I am grateful to Wren Sturdevant, Max Sturdevant, John Sturdevant, Elettra Cudignotto, Rachelle Dyer, Allan Mazur, Polly Mazur, Sophie Phillipson, Spencer Phillipson, Kelly Phillipson, Julie Tribe, Lisa Rhudy, Michael Ross, Jennie Goutet, Chuck Carter, Leslie Paladino, Jessica Santina, Sarah Hoggatt, Jun Kinoshita, Echo Davenport, David Campbell, and Rita Henderson for their help and encouragement.

I am also grateful to Sarina Jepsen, director of endangered species and aquatic conservation at the Xerces Society, who generously provided expert review.

About the Author

Rachel Mazur, PhD, is the author of *Speaking of Bears* (Globe Pequot, 2015), the award-winning picture book *If You Were a Bear* (Sequoia Natural History Association, 2008), and many articles for scientific and trade publications. She is passionate about writing stories to connect kids with nature—and inspiring them to protect it. Rachel lives with her husband and two children in El Portal, California, where she oversees the wildlife program at Yosemite National Park.

To learn more about The Nature Club series, please visit natureclubbooks.com.

To learn more about the art of Elettra Cudignotto, please visit elettracudignotto.com.

To learn more about the art of Rachelle Dyer, please visit rachellepaintings.com.

Made in the USA
Middletown, DE
22 December 2022